Hoot and Holler

D0541543

For my brother, Charlie – A.B.
For all my friends – R.R.

HOOT AND HOLLER
A Red Fox Book: 0 09 940898 8

First published in Great Britain by Hutchinson
An imprint of Random House Children's Books

Hutchinson edition published 2001
Red Fox edition published 2002

3 5 7 9 10 8 6 4

Text © Alan Brown 2001
Illustrations © Rimantas Rolia 2001

The right of Alan Brown and Rimantas Rolia
to be identified as the author and illustrator of this work
has been asserted in accordance with
the Copyright, Designs and Patents Act 1988

All rights reserved. No part of this publication may be reproduced,
stored in a retrieval system, or transmitted in any form or by any means,
electronic, mechanical, photocopying, recording or otherwise,
without the prior permission of the publishers.

Red Fox Books are published by Random House Children's Books,
61–63 Uxbridge Road, London W5 5SA,
a division of The Random House Group Ltd,
in Australia by Random House Australia (Pty) Ltd,
20 Alfred Street, Milsons Point, Sydney, NSW 2061, Australia,
in New Zealand by Random House New Zealand Ltd,
18 Poland Road, Glenfield, Auckland 10, New Zealand,
and in South Africa by Random House (Pty) Ltd,
Endulini, 5A Jubilee Road, Parktown 2193, South Africa

THE RANDOM HOUSE GROUP Limited Reg. No. 954009
www.kidsatrandomhouse.co.uk

A CIP catalogue record for this book is available from the British Library.

Printed in Singapore by Tien Wah Press [PTE] Ltd

Hoot and Holler

Alan Brown & Rimantas Rolia

RED FOX

Every night two owls played together in the Great Wood. The big owl was called Holler and the little owl was called Hoot.

They played swoop-and-snatch in the tumbling waterfall.

They played crouch-and-creep in the dripping cave.

They played glide-and-giggle round the
overgrown graveyard.

They loved the games they played, and
they loved each other, but they were afraid
to say how happy they were. Hoot was too
little and Holler was too shy.

One night when Holler wasn't looking,
a great gust of wind carried Hoot over
the graveyard wall and out of sight.

When Holler looked round, his friend was gone. Holler
thought Hoot did not want to play with a big owl any more.
Holler was sad, but was too shy to say so.

The storm got bigger and bigger and soon the wind
caught Holler too and blew him over the trees and far away.

When the storm was over, Hoot was on one side of the wood and Holler was on the other. The two owls flew through the night searching for each other. But the Great Wood was big and the night was dark. Hoot could not find Holler and Holler could not find Hoot.

Now Holler will never know that I loved playing with a big owl, thought Hoot.

Now Hoot will never know the fun I had playing with a little owl, thought Holler.

Holler flew to the middle of the Great Wood and asked Wise Owl, who lived in the hollow oak, 'Wise Owl, how can I find Hoot?'

Wise Owl blinked his eyes and said, 'You must call out, so Hoot can hear.'

'But I am too shy to call out all by myself in the Great Wood,' said Holler.

'You are big,' said Wise Owl, 'and you must be brave, or you will never find your friend.'

Holler flew to the spooky ruins where hares danced with their shadows. He called out softly but not very bravely, 'Hoot!'

Hoot was looking for Holler at the tumbling waterfall and did not hear Holler's shy call. Hoot was scared that Holler did not want to play with a little owl any more.

Hoo-oot!

Holler flew to the tall sycamore tree where foxes chased the mice in the rustly leaves. He called out softly but a little bit more bravely, 'Hoo-oot!'

Hoot was looking for Holler in the dripping cave, and still Holler's cry was not loud enough.

Holler realised that Wise Owl was right. Hoot would never hear a shy, soft call. Holler flew right to the top of the rocky crag and called out very bravely and very strongly,

Hoo-oot!

The moon came out from behind the clouds to see what the fuss was about. Silver badgers ran away in fright.

I love y

Hoot was looking for Holler in the overgrown
graveyard when the loud call came. At last he heard
and called back as loud and strong as a little owl could.

Foxes and bats, hares and deer, badgers and mice, all
the animals in the Great Wood looked up as Hoot
came flying through the dark night.

Hoot and Holler were so happy to find each other,
they hooted and hollered and
played till morning.

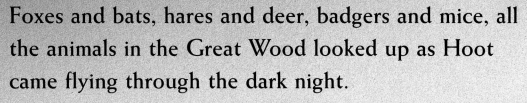

And they were never too shy to say,

'I'm happy'

'I'm sad'

'I'm scared'

or…

'I love you-hoo…'

Ever again.

More Red Fox picture books
for you to enjoy

ELMER
by David McKee 0099697203

MUMMY LAID AN EGG
by Babette Cole 0099299119

RUNAWAY TRAIN
by Benedict Blathwayt 0099385716

DOGGER
by Shirley Hughes 009992790X

WHERE THE WILD THINGS ARE
by Maurice Sendak 0099408392

OLD BEAR
by Jane Hissey 0099265761

MISTER MAGNOLIA
by Quentin Blake 0099400421

ALFIE GETS IN FIRST
by Shirley Hughes 0099855607

OI! GET OFF OUR TRAIN
by John Burningham 009985340X

GORGEOUS
by Caroline Castle and Sam Childs 0099400766